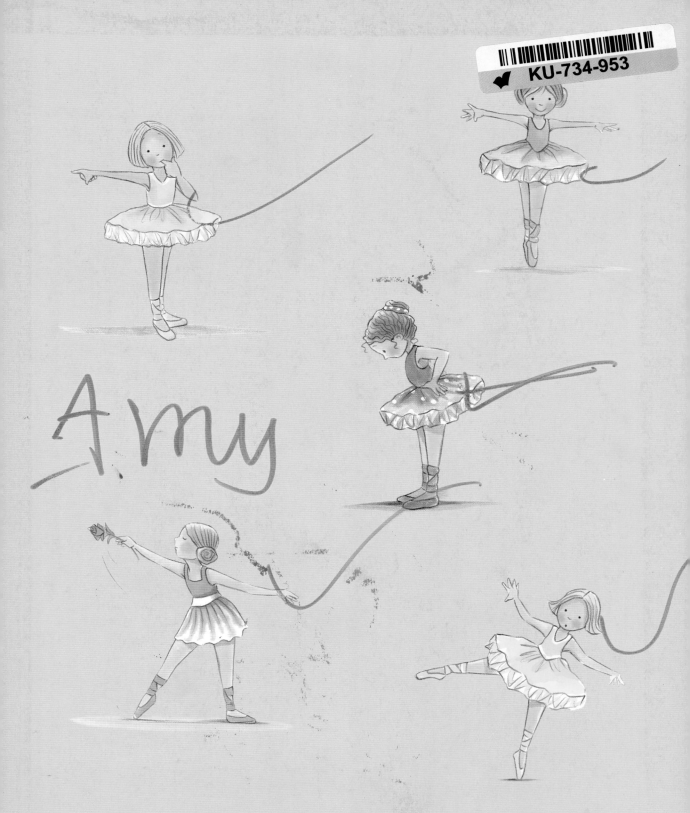

Amy

This book belongs to:

....

....

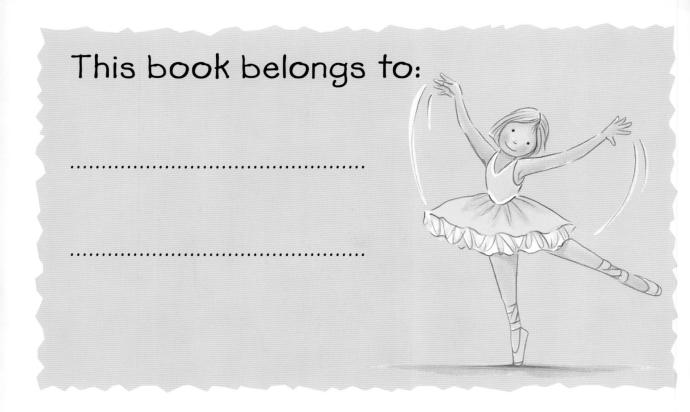

This edition published by Parragon in 2009

Parragon
Queen Street House
4 Queen Street
Bath BA1 1HE, UK

ISBN 978-1-4075-2154-1
Printed in China

Ballerinas are Beautiful

PaRragon

Bath New York Singapore Hong Kong Cologne Delhi Melbourne

Dizzy Ballerina Izzy

Izzy loves to ballet dance,
like lots of little girls.
She practises her steps each day.
She spins and jumps and twirls!

Izzy likes the music,
and the pretty costumes, too.
But twirling is her favourite thing.
It's what she loves to do.

But though she twirls so beautifully,
she has a problem, too.
"I can't tell *my* left from right!
Whatever can I do?"

When all the ballerinas
start dancing to the right,
Izzy dances to the left.
It happens every night!

"Watch where you are going!"
cried Ballerina Di.
"You keep treading on my toes,
when you go whirling by!"

Ballerina Zoe said,
"She really has to go.
Unless she learns her left and right,
she's going to spoil the show!"

"I give up!" poor Izzy sobbed,
and ran off then to hide.
"I wish I knew *my* left and right.
What can I do?" she cried.

"Don't be upset," said kindly Di.
"I know what to do,
to help you solve the problem.
Just give me your right shoe."

She tied a bell on to the toe,
and fixed it with a stitch.
"Now, when you hear it tinkle,
you'll know which foot is which!"

"How wonderful!" cried Izzy,
twirling to the right.
"Now I know which one is which,
I'd love to dance tonight!"

So Izzy wore her special shoe.
Her twirling stole the show!
"Now I can twirl up on the stage
and know which way to go!"

Shy Ballerina Di

Ballerina Di was as
dainty as can be.
No other ballerina
danced as daintily as she.

When she skipped with other girls,
holding hands together,
they said she danced as lightly
as a cloud or floating feather!

One day, the teacher told the class,
"There's going to be a show.
I want to give the leading role
to dainty Di, you know."

"I'm far too shy!" protested Di,
"I'd really rather not,
Already, I feel nervous –
my tummy's in a knot!"

Finally, the first night came,
but then disaster struck.
Zoe fell and hurt her foot.
It really was bad luck!

"You can't dance the lea
What ever shall we
Shy Di is the only
who knows the part

Shy Di looked at all her friends.
"I'll dance the part," she sighed.
"I can't let *my* friends down.
At least I will have tried!"

She trembled as the curtain rose,
but as the music played,
Di could not believe it!
"I just don't feel afraid!"

Di danced as she had never danced.
The crowd all called for more.
"What a dainty dancer!
She's a star, for sure!"

Showy Ballerina Zoe

Ballerina Zoe could
leap high off the ground,
and land so very gracefully,
she'd barely make a sound!

But though she was so graceful,
it went right to her head.
Instead of practising her steps,
she used to boast instead.

It made the other dancers cross.
"We're quite fed up with Zoe.
Why does she have to brag so much,
and be so proud and showy?"

One day, Zoe had some news.
"I've heard about a show.
There's going to be an audition.
I think we all should go!"

"I know that I will win a part.
Of that, you can be sure.
But you might get a little role,
if you would practise more."

The day of the audition came.
"I'll stretch and do some bends,
to warm up ready for the test,"
said Zoe to her friends.